This book is given with love:

_____

_____

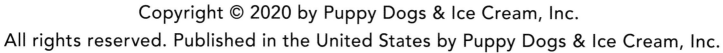

For all inquiries, please contact us at:
info@puppysmiles.org

To see more of our books, visit us at:
www.PuppyDogsAndIceCream.com

I CAN YELL LOUDER!

Author: Jennifer Gaither
Illustrator: CJ Centeno

There's a girl in my class,
whose name is Michelle...
And I've got to tell you,
she just loves to yell!

One sunny afternoon,
   my class went out to play...
We sat under a tree,
   enjoying the warm spring day.

It was all so great,
an afternoon dream...
But then the peace was shattered,
when Michelle began to scream.

The ballerinas stopped dancing,
  and the cows stopped mooing...
The deer stopped prancing,
  and even then cars stopped moving!

I was so tired of the noise,
 it was time for her to stop...
So I came up with a plan,
 before our eardrums would pop!

I walked up to Michelle,
   a big smile on my face...
But I stumbled and fell,
   I tripped on my shoelace!

I quickly stood up after tying my shoe,
and declared to Michelle, "I can yell louder than you!"
She scrunched up her face and let out a scream,
she yelled so loud her ears started to steam!

The clowns stopped joking,
   and the babies stopped crying...
The frogs stopped croaking,
   and even the birds stopped flying.

"That was nothing," I boasted,
and opened my mouth...
I let out a scream,
but no sound came out.

Michelle's eyes started to water,
as she laughed at the sight...
A scream with no sound,
just doesn't work right.

Michelle teased with a smirk,
    "You were quiet as a gnat!"
But I smiled with confidence,
    "Are you sure about that?"

"My scream was so loud,
it couldn't be heard!"
Michelle rolled her eyes,
"Well that's just absurd."

"Actually," I said, "it really is true.
     I guess it's just something you cannot do."
Michelle screamed so loud that it shook the whole school,
     it even made waves in the swimming pool!

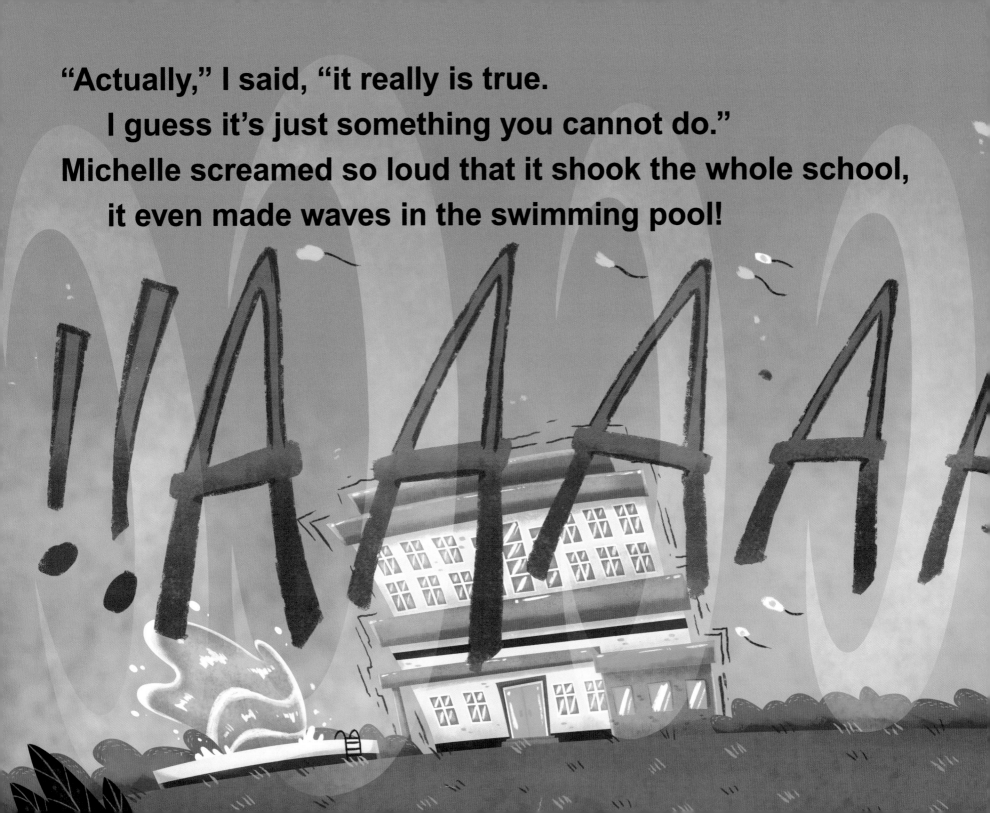

My sneaky plan was working,
   a silly scream with no sound...
Michelle's voice was getting tired,
   as the class gathered around.

Michelle is no longer,
   the loudest yeller in class...
She learned that yelling was silly,
   it's now a thing of the past!

What we've learned from Michelle,
    is a valuable lesson today...
Yelling's never the answer,
    when you don't get your way!

 **Claim Your FREE Gift!**

Visit ➡ PDICBooks.com/icanyell

Thank you for purchasing I Can Yell Louder!, and welcome to the Puppy Dogs & Ice Cream family.

We're certain you're going to love the little gift we've prepared for you at the website above.